THE AMAZING ADVENTURES OF THE DC SUPER-PETS!

Battle of the Super-Pets

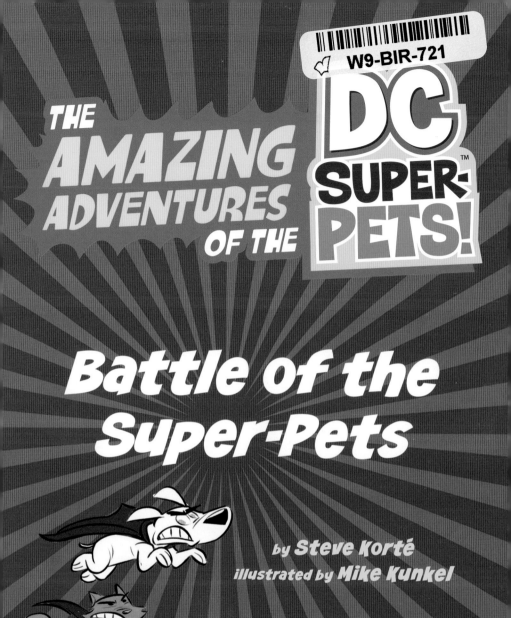

by **Steve Korté**

illustrated by **Mike Kunkel**

PICTURE WINDOW BOOKS
a capstone imprint

Published by Picture Window Books, an imprint of Capstone
1710 Roe Crest Drive
North Mankato, Minnesota 56003
capstonepub.com

Cataloging-in-Publication Data is available at the Library of Congress website
ISBN: 9781484672174 (hardcover)
ISBN: 9781484672136 (paperback)
ISBN: 9781484672143 (ebook PDF)

Summary: Best friends Streaky and Krypto are mad at each other.
They need to put their differences aside and join forces to save the day.

Designed by Elyse White

Printed and bound in China. PO# 5449

TABLE OF CONTENTS

He is Supergirl's furry friend.

He was once an ordinary cat.

He now has many of the same superpowers as Supergirl.

These are . . .

THE AMAZING ADVENTURES OF

Streaky the Super-Cat!

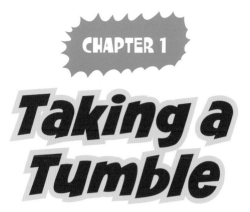

Taking a Tumble

Streaky the Super-Cat is taking a nap.

He is snoozing on a fluffy cloud high

above Midvale. He is dreaming of sushi.

Suddenly, Krypto the Super-Dog comes

crashing through the clouds.

Krypto is playing fetch. He is chasing

a metal pipe that Supergirl has thrown.

Streaky is still in a deep sleep as he falls

toward the ground.

He lands right on top of Krypto.

The startled cat is *very* annoyed.

Krypto is equally annoyed to have

the Super-Cat land on him.

Streaky and Krypto start wrestling.

They become a swirling ball of

superpowered rivals.

"Hey! Stop that!" says Supergirl.

"Instead of fighting, you two should use your superpowers in a friendly contest. Follow me!"

CHAPTER 2

A Friendly Contest

Supergirl and the pets fly to the edge of Midvale Lake. Supergirl easily picks up a massive metal chain that she finds on the shore.

"You can use this for a tug-of-war," she says.

Each pet grabs an end of the chain.

They pull on it with all their super-strength.

The chain breaks apart. Krypto flies

backward through the air. Streaky smiles

because he thinks he has won.

Not far away is a construction site. There is a ground-breaking ceremony for a new subway tunnel.

The mayor of Midvale has a shovel in her hands. She is about to dig the first hole in front of a crowd of people and photographers.

Just as the mayor lifts the shovel,

Krypto falls from the sky.

Krypto creates a giant hole in the ground! The crowd cheers for the Super-Dog. The mayor thanks Krypto for helping to dig such a large hole for the subway.

Krypto returns to the lake in triumph as a hero. Supergirl declares that the first round is a tie.

"Next up is a race to the other side of the lake and back," says Supergirl. "That will show which Super-Pet is the fastest! Go!"

Streaky runs on top of the water. Krypto zooms underwater along the bottom of the lake. Both pets end the race at the same time.

"It's another tie!" says Supergirl.

The two Super-Pets frown and

grumble at each other.

CHAPTER 3

Teamwork

Suddenly, Supergirl's super-hearing detects the sound of an alarm. It's going off at a bank in downtown Midvale.

She zooms into the air with the two pets right beside her. As they approach the bank, Supergirl ducks behind a cloud.

The Super-Pets keep flying to the bank. They discover Lex Luthor and his gang breaking into a vault!

Streaky uses his freeze-breath to create a giant block of ice around the villains' feet. They can't move!

Krypto grabs Luthor's collar in his mouth and lifts the villain into the air. "Put me down, you mangy mutt!" yells Luthor.

The two pets fly Luthor and his gang to the police station. Supergirl is waiting for them.

"It looks like both of you are more effective when you work *together*!" she says.

Streaky and Krypto smile and nod in agreement. They smack paws and are once again the best of friends.

AUTHOR!

Steve Korté is the author of many books for children and young adults. He worked at DC Comics for many years, editing more than 600 books about Superman, Batman, Wonder Woman, and the other heroes and villains in the DC Universe. He lives in New York City with his husband, Bill, and their super-cat, Duke.

ILLUSTRATOR!

Mike Kunkel wanted to be a cartoonist ever since he was a little kid. He has worked on numerous projects in animation and books, including many years spent drawing cartoon stories about creatures and super heroes such as the Smurfs and Shazam! He has won the Annie Award for Best Character Design in an Animated Television Production and is the creator of the two-time Eisner Award-winning comic book series Herobear and the Kid. Mike lives in southern California, and he spends most of his extra time drawing cartoons filled with puns, trying to learn new magic tricks, and playing games with his family.

"Word Power"

ceremony (SER-uh-moh-nee)—special actions, words, or music performed to mark an important event

detect (dih-TEKT)—to notice something

mangy (MEYN-jee)—dirty or gross

massive (MAS-iv)—large

rival (RYE-vuhl)—someone with whom you compete

subway (SUHB-way)—a system of trains that runs underground in a city

triumph (TRAHY-uhmf)—victory

vault (VAWLT)—a safe room or compartment to store things of value

WRITING PROMPTS

1. Streaky and Krypto are best friends and work well together. Write about a time you and your best friend teamed up and worked together.

2. Make a list of three ways Streaky and Krypto could have solved their fight on their own.

3. Pretend you are Streaky or Krypto. Write an apology note to your best friend.

DISCUSSION QUESTIONS

1. Which pet deserved to be mad at the beginning of the story? Both? Neither? Explain your answer.

2. Do you think the friendly competition was a good idea? Why or why not?

3. Why do you think Supergirl left the Super-Pets on their own?